Amy and Gully
with Aliens

W.W. Rowe
Illustrations by Adam Chow

Snow Lion Publications
Ithaca, New York

Snow Lion Publications
P. O. Box 6483
Ithaca, NY 14851 USA
(607) 273-8519
www.snowlionpub.com

Printed by McNaughton & Gunn
Saline, MI USA
August 2009

ISBN-10: 1-55939-328-9
ISBN-13: 978-1-55939-328-7

Library of Congress Cataloging-in-Publication Data

Rowe, William Woodin.
  Amy and Gully with aliens / W.W. Rowe ; illustrations by Adam Chow.
    p. cm.
  Summary: Amy and her brother Gully learn about the interconnectedness
of all life, selfless compassion, and the power of pure intention when they
are beamed aboard an alien spacecraft and enter a "movie" about a prince.
  ISBN-13: 978-1-55939-328-7 (alk. paper)
  ISBN-10: 1-55939-328-9 (alk. paper)
  [1. Fantasy. 2. Conduct of life—Fiction. 3. Extraterrestrial beings—Fiction.
4. Brothers and sisters—Fiction. 5. Buddhism—Fiction.] I. Chow, Adam,
ill. II. Title.
  PZ7.R7953Amt 2009
  [Fic]—dc22
                                                        2009027615

Amy and Gully with Aliens

For Eleanor

Acknowledgment

Part of this book is gratefully based on some teachings of Thich Nhat Hanh.

Contents

1

A Secret Mission

"Hey! Stop! STOP!"

Wildly waving his arms, Gully chased the bus, but it disappeared around the corner.

"Too late, Amy!" he called to his younger sister. "We'll have to get Dad to take us."

"He got pretty mad last time, Gully."

"Yeah, but this wasn't our fault. C'mon, hurry!"

Rarf! Ruff! Mr. Dryfield's basset hound Elmer yelped as they sped past his yard. He ran the entire length of the fence, as if trying to follow them on some exciting adventure.

Reaching home, they burst through the kitchen door. Mr. Trent peered over his newspaper. "Not again."

"The bus came early, Dad." Gully was breathing heavily. "We were there on time."

Mrs. Trent flipped a sizzling pancake on the stove. "I do think you've been cutting it too close."

"Today," said Mr. Trent, "is the last time I'm being your personal bus service. And you'll have to wait. I need to make some phone calls."

When he dropped them off, Amy and Gully went straight to the auditorium. The school meeting was still going on. Slipping into the back row, they saw the short, round body of Mrs. Clearpot, the biology teacher, facing the students. She wore a shimmery silver dress with a bright red belt.

". . . and so," Mrs. Clearpot was saying, "I was shocked —yes, that is not too strong a word—*shocked* when no one in the entire class could identify the leaf of a common, ordinary walnut tree." She paused. "Trees are our friends—even if they don't have the good sense to dress warmly in winter, hee hee." Her round body bobbed and swayed like a huge, silver balloon.

"Trees are like people. The trunks are their bodies. The branches, their arms. Each leaf is like a friendly little hand, waving in the breeze." Smiling and squinting, she waved a chubby hand at the students.

"Aw, come on!" a whiny voice whispered. It was Gerry Flathers, just in front of Amy and Gully. A few muffled giggles could be heard.

Mrs. Clearpot raised her voice. "Yes, trees are our

friends. They offer us a green umbrella against the summer's heat . . . and a glorious display of colors in the fall. How dare we insult them by failing to know their names! How do you think they must feel?"

"Pretty numb," Gerry Flathers croaked.

Laughter rippled across the room.

Mrs. Clearpot's glasses flashed in the light. "A few of you seem to think that is funny. Well, life can take strange, amazing forms. *Very* amazing forms.

"You children probably like to watch movies about aliens. Well, why don't you pretend that trees are alien beings? Pretend you are on a secret mission to observe them . . . and bring back interesting alien samples. Your assignment is to bring five different leaves to school. Tomorrow morning, I will call on some of you to come up here and say their names. So you had better be prepared."

Mr. Wilkins, the principal, stepped forward. "Thank you, Mrs. Clearpot. I'm sure everyone will carry out this *secret mission*, as you so inspiringly put it. Learning can be fun, if we just cooperate. You may go to your classrooms now, but I would like to see Gerald Flathers in my office immediately."

When the bus dropped them off after school, Amy asked what happened to Gerry Flathers.

"He wouldn't say," Gully replied. "He just frowned and turned red."

They walked in silence for a while. "Let's help each other get the leaves," Amy said.

Gully laughed scornfully. "That was *soo* dumb." He squinted his eyes, straining a wide smile. "Pretend it's a secret mission, children. And bring me interesting alien samples."

"At least she tries, Gully."

"She tries, all right." He rolled his eyes. "We can get maple leaves in the backyard, but we'll have to go to the park for the others."

"Let's do it now," said Amy, "so we don't forget."

"Okay."

Turning right, they entered Rosedale Park. The jogging path curved up a grassy slope between tall trees.

Gully pointed to the left. "You take that side. Get two of each kind. We can sort them out later."

Amy had trouble reaching some of the branches. Under one tree was a clump of pale blue flowers with blossoms like little bells. Bending down, she tilted one up gently with her finger. "Gully, look!"

"What?"

"C'mere, quick! I don't know what it is!"

Gully ran over, but stopped short. "We're looking for leaves, not flowers," he said angrily.

"No, look!" Amy pointed to a tiny red speck, floating just above the bell-shaped blossoms.

"We're not looking for bugs, either. Why don't you—" Gully's mouth dropped open. The tiny red speck was now the size of a dime, only thicker. Suddenly, it rose straight up and hovered between their faces.

"Yow! That was fast!" Gully reached out to grab it, but the red dime jumped sideways. He blinked in amazement. It looked like a large cherry lollipop.

"Eee, Gully! It's growing!"

Before their eyes, the red lollipop became the size of a thick, red frisbee. Rising straight up, it spread out like a giant umbrella! It almost blotted out the sky! They were standing in the shadow of a huge flying saucer!

Amy gaped, terrified. Gully helplessly raised one arm as a wide, bright beam shot down from the saucer. Caught in its dazzling white light, they were lifted gently upwards, their eyes closed, like two lifeless statues. One end of the saucer separated, forming a shadowy hole . . .

It was into this hole that Amy and Gully, floating up as if through clear water, disappeared. After that,

the saucer shrank back to a tiny red speck and continued to hover quietly among the bell-shaped flowers.

2

The Snoods

Gully's head felt thick and groggy. He seemed to be floating up out of a deep sleep. He vaguely remembered a little red bug, flying above some bell-shaped flowers. But where was he now? Could this be a dream? Somewhere nearby, he heard rough, fuzzy voices.

"Dorg! The prisoners are now strapped down."

"Not so loud, Ra! We are tuned to their language channel, and the sleep-ray will soon wear off. Already they could be conscious."

"No matter. They look weak. The straps will hold."

"Be not sure! The creatures from Andrus Four also looked weak, yet they broke the straps. We must stay careful."

With a great effort, Gully opened his eyes. Above him was a creamy-green ceiling. He was lying on a table, arms and legs tied down. He tried to move, but the straps held him like iron hands.

All of a sudden, Gully heard a slithery, scraping noise. He pretended to be asleep, and the fuzzy voices continued.

"Dorg! They have no eyes on the ends of their eye-stalks! The stalks resemble ours, but—"

"Those are fingers, you fool! They use them to hold and to feel. See, Ra, each being has only two flap-covered eyes, set in the hairy bulb at the top of its body."

"How primitive! They cannot see behind them."

"Yes, Ra. Look. They have only four arms. The ends of the lower two arms are covered by walking pads."

Gully was still weak and groggy. Opening his eyes again, he saw something round and shiny. *Yow! What was that?*

The creature looked like a silver octopus. It stood on four glittery tentacles. Up above, four thinner ones waved gently in the air. Its body—or head—was like a big silver ball with a glowing red ring around the middle. On top of the ball stood five fingerlike stalks, each with a bulging eye.

Gully stared in horror. Off to the side, another silver creature swayed before a wide control panel. Its tentacles were pressing keys and turning dials.

Behind him, Gully heard a weak moan, followed by a rustling sound. "Eee, Gully! Octo-pusses!"

Turning his head, he saw Amy, wide-eyed, lying on another table. "Help!" she cried, struggling frantically. "I can't move!"

"We're tied down, Amy." Gully twisted back towards the creatures. "Who are you?" he asked helplessly. "Where are we?"

The creatures blinked their red rings. "We are Snoods," said one. "You are on a rish," said the other. Their fuzzy voices sounded strangely hollow.

"A rish?" Gully's head was spinning. "What's that?"

Reaching up, the Snood called Ra pressed a purple button just below his eyestalks. "Rish," he said. There was a click and a whirring sound. Then a squeaky little voice inside him replied: "Flying ship. Spacecraft."

"But why are we here?"

"You make stupid questions," said the Snood called Dorg. "You here for zarbites."

"What are zarbites?" Amy anxiously asked. "Do they hurt?"

Pressing his purple button again, Ra said: "Zarbites." After a click and a whir, the squeaky little voice replied: "Laboratory tests. Experiments."

"Eee, Gully! They're gonna speriment on us!" Amy burst into tears.

"Don't cry, Amy." Gully tried to sound brave and confident. "I'll think of something."

"What?" said Dorg.

"Yes," said Ra. "What will you think?"

Both Snoods scurried over to Gully's table, excitedly waving their tentacles. "What?" they repeated. "Tell us! Tell us now!" They sounded desperately curious.

A sly smile crept across Gully's face. "I can't. It's a secret."

"What mean secret?" Ra demanded.

"Translate, you fool!" cried Dorg. "Quickly!"

Pressing another button, a black one this time, Ra

hurriedly said: "Secret." After a click and a whir, the squeaky little voice replied: "Fuzzle. Grizmist."

"Tell!" shouted the Snoods. "You tell fuzzle! You tell us grizmist!" They hopped impatiently up and down.

Gully grinned slyly. "I might . . . if you take off these straps."

"Okay. Yes. Sure," said Ra. "Then you tell us grizmist." He began to unfasten Gully's leg-straps.

"No, Ra! Wait!" Dorg's red ring was blinking rapidly. "Could be trick!"

"Yes, Dorg. You are right. We must give prisoners zarbites."

"Gully! Don't let them!" Amy tugged violently at her straps.

"You not worry," said Dorg. "No prisoner ever die from zarbites. So far."

"So far!" Gully yelled. "You mean it could kill us?"

"You not worry. Many creatures on your planet. You die—we get other prisoners—give them zarbites. Ra, prepare sleep-ray. I bring chortalizer."

"Eee, Gully! Stop them!"

"I can't, Amy!" Gully wildly twisted his neck. "Wait, Snoods! WAIT!"

Dorg was already clutching a purple box with crystal tubes and a pale pink screen. "Chortalizer is ready. Ra, activate sleep-ray!"

"Yes, Dorg." Pointing one glittery tentacle at Amy and another at Gully, Ra pressed a blue button just above his red ring.

Zik-zik! Kcherassh! There was a double yellow flash and a sound like lightning piercing the air. Just before they fell asleep, Amy and Gully could see the eyestalks of both Snoods curving over them.

3

Zarbites

Amy woke up first. Her head was swirling with pictures. She saw herself in her grandmother's attic, putting on a red wig. But suddenly the red wig was a red frisbee, flying over some little blue flowers. That was crazy!

Amy blinked her eyes. She was lying on the same table, her arms and legs strapped down.

"Gully!" she whispered. "Are you awake?"

Gully made no sound, so she turned her head to look for the Snoods.

One silver creature stood before the control panel. The other held a pear-shaped bottle filled with smoky liquid.

Amy blinked. Her head was swirling again. Now she was pouring chocolate sauce over her vanilla ice cream . . . but the chocolate sauce jumped up and barked, because it was Elmer, Mr. Dryfield's basset hound, who got very excited when she and Gully ran home after missing the bus.

Amy struggled against the straps. "Gully! Wake up!"

There was no answer. Amy glared indignantly at the Snoods. "Hey, you octo-pusses! What did you do to us?"

Ra scurried over to Amy's table. "Just zarbites. Routine zarbites."

Dorg twisted his eyestalks. "We make memory scan. You feeling aftereffects."

Amy shuddered. "That's not nice. Snooping into our memories. We were asleep . . . and helpless. Gully! Wake up!"

"Hunh?"

"Those awful Snoods mixed up our memories. Are you okay?"

"Yeah, I guess so. Just groggy and tired. Yow! I feel like I'm seeing a hundred things at once!"

"I told you. They mixed up our memories."

"Not mix up," said Dorg. "Just scan. On chortalizer screen. You soon see normal."

"I hope so," said Amy. "I'm very thirsty."

Ra rubbed two tentacles together uncertainly. "What mean thirsty?"

"I want something to drink," said Amy. "Have you any juice or milk?"

"What mean juicermilk?"

"They don't understand, Amy." Gully lifted his head as high as he could. "Amy needs water."

Dorg raised three tentacles in amazement. "Ra scanned your needs when we capture you. No water-need indicated." He aimed his eyestalks at Ra. "You make wrong scan, clumsy idiot! How can I work control panel and run scanner too? I only have eight arms!"

"You sometimes clumsy too, Dorg. Who make us go down instead of up when we fly over Korba Nine? Who almost make rish go crashing into mountain? So ha ha to you, Dorg."

"Dare not to laugh, Ra. I remember when you—"

"Please!" Amy interrupted. "I need some water."

Dorg blinked his red ring. "Zarbites reveal your bodies are mostly water anyway. Better you dry out."

"No!" cried Amy. "We'll die! We've got to have water! Please!"

"Such needs very primitive," said Dorg. "But okay. Ra, get skidger. Reverse plando on chortalizer."

"Yes, Dorg. I do." Ra scuttled to a low cabinet and pulled out a blue tube. Fastening one end to the purple box, he dangled the other over Amy's face. "You open mouth."

Amy bravely parted her lips. The tube clicked against her teeth. It felt strangely light. Ra twisted some dials on the box, and it made a gushing, bubbly sound.

Amy tasted something sugary-sweet. "Umm," she murmured. "Strawberry soda, only better. Try some, Gully! It's like drinking strawberry candy!"

She blinked her eyes. "Hey! Look at those big red dolls! They're bouncing and dancing. They're really fun-ee!" Amy giggled, but it was more like a gurgle because she was still drinking.

Dorg yanked out the blue tube. "Ra, you fool! You reverse glander, not plando. You produce porzy instead of water. Prisoner seeing dream-pictures."

"No matter, Dorg. Need for liquid satisfied. Time to finish zarbites."

"Wait!" cried Gully. "You might hurt us! You already did your zarbites!"

"That's okay, Gull-ee! Whee! Climb on this flying elephant! Have some strawberry soda!"

Gully struggled frantically. What could he do? Amy didn't even seem to care!

The Snoods scurried closer, hovering above them, eyestalks curving down. Ra raised two gently waving tentacles.

Gully pulled in desperation against the straps, but

they held him fast. He shuddered, gritting his teeth
. . .

Zik-zik! Kcherassh! Once again, a double yellow
flash, followed by the sound of striking lightning. The
two prisoners, lying flat on their tables, instantly lost
consciousness.

4

A Plan

Gully slowly opened his eyes. The Snoods were leaning over Amy, scanning the chortalizer screen.

"Look, Dorg! Smaller creature also has talent for sudden trickery. Can be devious and sly."

"You are right, Ra. When prisoners awaken, they maybe try to trick us. I watch larger creature. You keep an eye on smaller one."

"Yes, Dorg." Ra raised a tentacle up to one of his eyestalks. *Popp!* Coming loose, the eye made an explosive, snapping sound. He carefully placed it on Amy's chest.

"Ra, you idiot! In their language, to keep an eye on something means to watch it closely. You have the brains of a moon crater."

"Sorry, Dorg." Ra picked up his eye and popped it back on the end of its stalk.

"Focus chortalizer on both creatures again."

"I focus, Dorg."

The Snoods turned towards Gully. Quickly he shut his eyes, pretending to be asleep.

"Prisoners have puny lifespan. They will live less than three durons."

"Yes, Ra. Little sense in testing them. Zarbites show low capacity for reading minds and changing matter."

"Wait, Dorg! Look at screen. Prisoners have high capacity for loving-kindness. But also for selfishness. Will sometimes say false things."

"Yes, Ra. Be not careless when they awaken. Remember how the oily-tongued beings from Zarkon Seven deceived you? They flattered you until you showed off all your buttons. Even your red off-button, you shiny fool! I had to start you again."

"Insult me not, Dorg. You too were deceived by their praise. Remember? You showed off dangerously with control panel. You are the greater fool!"

"Not so, Ra. But stay silent. We must finish zarbites before sleep-ray wears off."

Gully kept his eyes closed. The tests didn't really hurt, but once he felt tiny prickles in his chest.

Soon Ra's voice said:s "Zarbites completed."

Gully could hear them scuttling away. He opened his eyes. Both Snoods stood before the control panel.

The purple box was attached to the panel by a thick, white cord.

"Hey," Gully whispered. "Are you awake?"

Amy sighed happily. "You are sooo silly," she said softly. "You can stay here in my room. Mom and Dad won't mind. It'll be fun-ee!"

"Amy! Wake up! You're dreaming. It's that stuff you drank. Amy!"

"Wha? Who?" Amy's eyes fluttered open. "Oh, Gully! Did you see those dolls? They were wearing pink and red pajamas! They bounced like balloons!"

"It was a dream, Amy. Now listen. I've got a plan!"

Ra scuttled over. "What plan?" he asked.

"Yes," Dorg demanded. "You tell us what plan."

"None of your business," said Gully. "Anyway, it's a secret."

"No more pretend fuzzle!" cried Dorg. "No more pretend grizmist!" He blinked his red ring very fast. "Be not tricky! We have results of zarbites. We know all things you can do."

"All things?" Gully asked doubtfully. "I'll bet you didn't see us *grockle*."

Both Snoods grew intensely quiet.

Dorg curled two tentacles together like twisted vines. "How you grockle?" he demanded.

"Yes," said Ra. "Show us!"

"No." Gully shook his head. "It's very special. When we grockle, our faces turn blue, and—"

"Gully! We can't—"

"Yes we can, Amy. Did you forget? Mom and Dad said we're both old enough to grockle. Think! *Think*, and you'll remember."

"Oh, uh . . . yes." Amy tried not to look puzzled. "I remember now. We *are* old enough to grockle."

"What else happen?" Dorg demanded. "After faces turn blue."

Gully grinned. "Our bodies change shape."

"What shape?" said Ra.

"Oh, a surprise shape." Gully tried not to laugh.

"What mean surprise?" asked Dorg. He pointed his eyestalks at Ra. "Translate! Quickly!"

Pressing his black button, Ra hurriedly said "Surprise." After a click and a whir, the squeaky little voice replied: "Ohzoop. Farshock."

Both Snoods jumped up and down, waving their tentacles. "Show! Show how you grockle!"

Gully hesitated. "Well, okay. But only if you show us the results of the zarbites."

"Yes. Sure. Right," said Ra.

"Wait!" cried Dorg. "You grockle first. *Then* we show results. We are not fooled, so ha ha to you."

"Okay," Gully grinned. "You win. Let us stand up, and we'll grockle. We have to do it together."

"Yes. Sure." Ra unfastened Gully's straps, while Dorg undid Amy's . . .

5

A Problem

Gully slid off the table. "All right, Amy. Come over here and we'll grockle. Give us some room, Snoods!"

Amy jumped down and stood beside Gully. The Snoods crawled backwards expectantly. Their ten eyes glittered with curiosity.

"Make faces turn blue!" said Ra, dancing excitedly on his lower tentacles. "Do it now!"

"Yes!" cried Dorg. "Then make bodies change shape! Change into surprise! Ohzoop! Farshock!" His eyestalks strained forward eagerly. "You grockle now!"

"Hang on," said Gully. "We have to get ready."

"How we hang on?" said Ra. He wrapped three tentacles around a ceiling beam, letting his body swing free like a silver balloon. "Like this?"

"You stupid comet-tail!" cried Dorg. "To hang on means to wait in their language."

Ra dropped to the floor. "Sorry, Dorg. Is painful to wait. Is difficult to wonder what farshock will be!"

"Yes, Ra. Is difficult." Dorg pointed two twitchy tentacles at Gully. "Why you take so long to prepare?"

"We're almost ready." Gully leaned his head close to Amy's. "Whatever I say," he whispered, "you shout something silly. Act goofy, too. And move up close to the Snoods."

"Why, Gully?" Amy shuddered. "They might—"

"Shush. Trust me. Then, when I say . . . *Kung Fu* . . . push Ra's red button as fast as you can. Understand?"

"Sure, Gully, but—"

"All right, Snoods," Gully announced in a solemn voice. "We will now begin the Secret Grockle Ceremony." With a smooth, fancy swoop, he placed one hand on his head.

"Cheeseburger!" he shouted, hopping on one leg.

Trying to look serious, Amy put one hand on her head and cried: "Ketchup!" She hopped like crazy.

The Snoods leaned forward, all ten eyes bulging, but nothing happened.

Gully raised his other hand. "Jellybean!" Swaying and spinning, he danced closer to the Snoods. "Yah! Yah! Yah!"

Trying not to giggle, Amy raised her other hand

and cried: "Gumdrop!" She also danced closer. "Eee-yah! Eee-yah!"

The Snoods raised their tentacles expectantly. Again, nothing hapened.

"Grockle not work," said Ra. "Faces not turn blue."

"Silence, Ra! Do not meddle and spoil the effect!"

"Yes, Dorg. Sorry. I not spoil."

"Thaagh!" Gully stuck out his tongue. "Bugs . . . Bunny!" He lurched towards Dorg.

"Thig!" Amy shouted. "Porky Pig!" She staggered up to Ra.

Clearing his throat, Gully shouted: "Kung . . . Fu!"

As he reached out to push Dorg's red button, Amy quickly pushed Ra's.

The Snoods, all eyes bulging, were frozen on the spot. Their rings stopped glowing. Their tentacles stopped waving. They stood there, motionless, like two glittery Christmas trees.

"Amy! We did it!" Gully smiled triumphantly. "Okay, you Snoods. Listen carefully. We'll never start you up again unless you promise to take us home right away. Understand?"

The Snoods remained motionless and silent.

"They can't talk, Gully." Amy looked worried. "Maybe they can't even hear you. Oh, no!" she gasped. "What'll we do now?"

"Snoods! Snoods! Take us home, or I'll . . ." Gully gave up, unable to think of a good threat.

"Their rings went out, Gully. They can't do anything." Amy glanced wildly at the control panel. "They can't fly the ship!"

"Don't worry, Amy. We'll figure out how to—"

"The ship's gonna crash! I know it!" Amy burst into tears.

"Don't cry. It's on automatic pilot. It *must* be. I'll figure out how to run it."

Amy kept sobbing. "We're . . . gonna . . . crash."

Gully rushed over to the control panel. Amy followed, sniffling. They stared helplessly at the dials, keys, and switches.

"Yow!" said Gully. "We'd better turn one of the Snoods back on. I'll keep my finger near his off-button just in case."

"Okay." Amy's face brightened. "Which button starts them?"

"I . . . I don't know!"

Amy started sobbing again.

"Don't cry, Amy. I'll press them all, one at a time." Gully tried to sound confident. "There aren't that many. It won't take—"

He was interrupted from behind by a strange noise.

Amy and Gully both jumped. It sounded like peals of musical laughter.

6
Mala

Startled, Amy and Gully turned away from the control panel. The musical laughter had come from a luminous figure in the doorway.

It looked like a man, molded out of golden clay. His smooth, radiant skin reminded Amy of a jar of honey on the kitchen window sill, with the morning sun shining through it. His eyes shone like two glittery diamonds.

As the golden man stepped forward, his leg stretched out through the air. Amazingly, it arched all the way over to Amy and Gully. Pulling up the other leg, he suddenly stood beside them.

"Eee, Gully! He's made of rubber!"

Peals of musical laughter rang out once more.

"Do not be afraid," said the golden man. His voice was calm and pleasant.

"Who are you?" Gully asked.

"You may call me Mala," he answered. "I intended to be here sooner, but I was occupied with communications." His piercing eyes shifted to the Snoods, who stood like silver statues near the wall. "I see, however, that you can take care of yourselves."

Amy wondered if he was angry because they had turned off the Snoods.

"It probably served them right," said the golden man, as if reading her mind. "The Snoods, I am sorry to say, are not terribly intelligent. A slight defect when they were constructed."

Gully stared. "You mean they're just machines?"

"Well, yes," said Mala. "Like what you call robots or androids. But these two Snoods were programmed to have emotions. Curiosity was overdone." He sighed. "They are sometimes foolishly curious. Particularly Ra. And Dorg is a bit too bossy. I trust they caused you no pain?"

"Uh, no," said Gully. "But those straps pinched a little."

"Well, you won't be on the tables anymore." With one arching step, the golden man stood beside the purple box. His diamond eyes scanned the pale pink screen. "You both have the potential for further testing. But first, I shall reactivate these sad-looking statues."

Two of Mala's fingers lept through the air. Zooming across the room, they struck like snakes, firmly pressing a yellow button on each Snood.

The shiny, round creatures came back to life. They waved their tentacles wildly, eyestalks curving in all directions.

"What was!?" cried Dorg. "Who dare to press off-button?"

"These weak, helpless prisoners outwitted you." The luminous man laughed. It sounded like chimes.

Ra waved two tentacles angrily. "Prisoners very tricky. Not strong but sneaky." He turned to Dorg.

"Mala look glorious and grand. Look better in prisoner shape than prisoners."

Dorg's eyestalks twisted back and forth. "Yes, Ra."

"What does he mean?" Gully asked.

"This is not my usual form," said the golden man. "I always take on a shape similar to that of our . . . guests. So as not to frighten them."

Amy's eyes grew wide. "What do you really look like?" she asked.

Mala hesitated. "My normal form has three heads and six arms. To your eyes, they would seem to be floating on fire." He turned to the Snoods. "Enough bungling. Go collect some plant samples. There is a well-kept garden below us on the surface of the planet."

"Yes, Mala."

"Yes, Mala."

The shiny creatures scuttled away.

Mala led Amy and Gully into a small, dark blue room. It was empty and bare, with a large, dark screen on one wall.

"Gully, look! A big TV!"

Mala's musical laugh rang out. "Not exactly." As he spoke, the screen became huge, and the room was suddenly larger.

Amy gaped in amazement. "It's a movie screen now!"

"Yow!" cried Gully. "This room keeps growing. But that's impossible. How big is this ship, anyway?"

Mala smiled. "Right now, it is the size of a tiny red speck. But here, we need it to be larger."

Gully's head was spinning. "You mean the ship is different sizes, inside and out?"

"I suppose you could call it that." Mala's eyes glittered. "You have much to learn about controlling matter. Also, about your true nature."

"Why are you testing us?" Gully asked.

"You will understand, but only after the tests. Now, if you will just—"

"Mala! Mala!" Both Snoods came scuttling through the door. Ra looked the same, but Dorg was much smaller. He was holding a big pink rose in his tentacles.

"I start to collect plants," the smaller Dorg said. "But monster chase me. Was fault of Ra. He make blunder. Ra, you are clumsy crater-brain!"

"Not my fault!" cried Ra. "Dorg make wrong readings. Dorg, you are stupid asteroid!"

Mala raised a luminous arm.

The Snoods fell silent, all eyes glaring at each other.

"Calm down," Mala commanded. "Tell me what happened."

"Was blunder of Ra," said Dorg. "He beam me down to collect plants. But he make me too small. I land on top of monster. Loud, brown monster. Monster make jumps and leaps. I fall off monster's back. Monster make roar. Also say *rarf*."

"Hey!" cried Gully. "I'll bet that was Elmer. You landed on Elmer, in Mr. Dryfield's yard."

"Yes!" Amy laughed. "Mr. Dryfield has beautiful roses."

"What mean roses?" asked Ra. His tentacles quivered excitedly.

"Yes!" said Dorg. "And what mean Elmer?"

Mala fixed Dorg with his diamond eyes. "The plant you are holding is called a rose. You Snoods must have incompletely programmed your language banks. And Elmer is clearly the name of a dog—a tame but loud animal who, *fortunately*, cannot report what he saw."

Mala laughed. "A big dog and a little Dorg. That's quite amusing. But enough mistakes. Ra, restore Dorg to his normal size. And you, Dorg, put the rose into a life-sustaining jar."

The Snoods waved their tentacles respectfully.

"Yes, Mala."

"Yes, Mala."

"And no more arguing. Now go. We need to get on with the tests."

Both Snoods scurried out the door, leaving Amy and Gully to wonder what their new tests would be.

7

Twins

"Sit down," Mala invited when the Snoods were gone. "The floor is soft now."

Amy and Gully dropped down onto the dark-blue surface. It was, indeed, as soft as a thick carpet.

"Good. Now, if you will face the screen, we can begin." Mala flashed his diamond eyes, and the wide screen suddenly lit up.

"Gully, look!"

Before them rose the milk-white towers of a splendid palace. Dark red banners rippled from its spires. In the very center, reflecting the sun, loomed a gold, onion-shaped dome.

"Wow!" said Gully. "How would you like to live there?"

The palace was surrounded by pink and white gardens. Marble fountains shot up arcs of rainbow spray.

The picture zoomed in to a sunny room inside the palace. A woman in purple robes and ruby earrings leaned over a fancy bed.

On the bed were two babies in pale blue garments. They lay side by side on cream-colored pillows with gold tassels. Behind the bed stood two other women, slowly fanning the air with long, silver paddles. One of the babies smiled peacefully in his sleep.

"Look, Gully! Isn't he cute?"

Gully yawned. "Uh, yeah, Amy."

The other baby smiled too, but it was not a pleasant smile. His delicate lips curled back in a way that seemed almost evil. The woman in purple robes drew back, horrified.

A tall, bearded man strode into the room. He wore a blue silk shirt, billowy pants, and gold shoes. "How is it with our sons?" he asked.

"Prince David is sleeping happily. But Prince Dargon is having a bad dream."

The bearded man shuddered. "May this not be a bad omen." Frowning, he left the room.

"How come those people speak our language?" Gully asked.

Mala raised a luminous hand. "The tests are set up that way. Please watch."

The picture zoomed back to the palace gardens, where two boys were playing. Amy and Gully could see that they were already three or four years old. They wore light blue playsuits and gold shoes. Kneeling on the pebbled path, David was building a little house with red and yellow sticks. He placed the painted sticks across each other with great care.

Dargon stood behind him, sniffing the air. He grinned unpleasantly. When the house was finished, he jumped forward with both feet, crushing it.

Amy gasped.

David looked up with a sad expression.

Laughing maliciously, Dargon snatched up two handfuls of white pebbles. Slowly he opened his hands. The pebbles rained evenly down on David's head.

"Fight back!" cried Gully. "He doesn't even fight back."

"Yii!" Dargon's eyes grew wide. His hand flew up to his neck. "Something stung me," he whined. "Where did it go?"

The next picture showed a richly furnished room. The two boys sat at a marble table, drawing with colored pencils. They looked a year or two older.

Dargon reached for a crystal jar. Lifting the lid, he

grabbed a handful of lemon candies. He offered some to David, who shook his head and kept on drawing.

Dargon ate two candies. He seemed to be sniffing the air. Then a sly smile appeared on his sticky-wet lips. He scattered the rest of the candy across the table and began drawing again.

An ugly, bulldog-faced man entered the room. He wore a white turban. Striding to the table, he pointed to the lemon candies. "Who took these?" he demanded.

"David did, Kamir." Dargon looked up with a sweet, innocent expression. "He wanted me to eat some too, but I refused."

David looked shocked.

Kamir scowled darkly. "Prince David! Hold out your hand."

Trembling slightly, David held out the palm of his right hand. Kamir brandished a wooden ruler in the air. "It is wrong to steal," he said. "Very wrong." Then he struck the boy sharply on his outstretched hand.

"No!" Amy cried. "That's not fair!"

"Aiieee!" Dargon slapped his cheek. "Cursed bee," he said. "That hurt."

David said nothing. He gingerly closed his fingers over the red welt. Two glistening tears slid down his face.

"Finish your drawings," Kamir ordered, sinking into a comfortable chair.

Dargon glared sideways at his brother as if to say, "Next time, maybe you'll eat some too." His mean smile slowly faded away . . .

The next picture showed the palace gardens. David, who looked much older now, stood beside a marble bench. A squirrel and a grey rabbit sat in the grass nearby.

David fed the rabbit a large piece of lettuce. Nibbling contentedly, the rabbit edged closer.

"Look, Gully! It's so tame!" Amy smiled happily. "I wish we had a pet like that."

Feeding the squirrel some nuts, David smiled warmly. He gently stroked the squirrel's dark grey fur.

Three white birds glided down, landing on the path. They had scruffy heads and round, black eyes. Looking up at David, they opened their beaks. He placed a small piece of bread in each one.

Zwisst! A stone sailed through the air. It just missed the birds. They took off, frantically flapping their wings.

The squirrel raced away into some bushes. But the rabbit froze, his nose twitching. He seemed paralyzed with fright. The next stone, a larger one, struck him directly on the head.

A triumphant laugh rang out. Dargon appeared, holding a wooden slingshot. The rabbit lay unconscious in the grass, his head oozing blood.

"Oh, no!" cried Amy. "He's dead."

"Yii!" Dargon wildly waved his arm. "Blasted bee!" he snarled. "Stung me on the back."

David reached down and felt the rabbit's soft, rounded chest. Carefully lifting the animal up, he turned to face his brother. There was great sadness in his eyes. "You are hurting yourself," he said. "But you do not know it."

Dargon drew back, strangely frightened. Then his face turned grim. "Give him to me," he said. "I'll finish him off."

"No." David cradled the rabbit in his arms. "I think he can be saved."

Dargon's eyes burned with anger. "I'll get you punished," he said. "Just wait."

Amy turned to Mala. "I can never see those bees. They must be awful small."

Mala laughed his musical laugh. "Perhaps there are no bees," he said.

"What do you mean?" said Gully.

"You and Amy have very strong feelings. A strong emotion can sometimes sting like a bee."

Gully's mouth dropped open. "You mean . . . you mean *we* made Dargon have those stings? That's impossible!"

"There is much you do not know about the tests," Mala declared. "You can indeed influence the beings on the screen—in some ways."

Gully blinked in disbelief. "But that means we can change what we are watching!"

Mala smiled. "Perhaps you *always* do," he said. "Though much less strongly than you can in this test. Please continue to watch."

8

The Necklace

Amy and Gully faced the screen. They saw a bright orange sunrise, reflected in the palace windows. Two soldiers in green uniforms guarded the arched marble door. Not far away, a fat man held two snowy-white horses by the reins. The man had a wide, bulging nose.

"Let's see if we can make his nose itch," Gully whispered.

"Okay!" Amy giggled. "Maybe he'll scratch it."

They both wished for the man's nose to itch, but he only blinked his eyes and yawned.

The palace door swung open. The tall, bearded man appeared. "I shall be riding alone this morning, Abdul."

"Yes, Sire." The fat man bowed.

The bearded man mounted his white horse and rode away into the sunrise . . .

The orange sun blended into a large, peach-colored bedroom. The wide bed, with its tall wooden frame and filmy white curtains, looked like an old sailing ship. The Queen stretched out on a couch near the window, pulling a golden spread across her body.

For a few moments, all was quiet. Then the door opened. Dargon sneaked into the room. His eyes were fixed on his mother's dressing table against the wall. Rushing past the bed, he went straight to the table and picked up an emerald necklace.

On the couch, the Queen lay very still beneath her golden spread, but she watched him closely. The boy held the necklace up to the light. It gleamed brightly. His lips curled in a tight smile. Slipping the necklace into his pocket, he left the room.

The Queen threw aside her spread. She tiptoed after Dargon. He hurried to a room at the back of the palace. His mother listened outside the door.

"Ah! What a beautiful necklace."

"Yes, Kamir. See how it gleams? I'll let you have it if you'll help me blame someone."

"Of course, my lad. Which servant do you wish to see beaten this time?"

"This time, Kamir, it must be my brother David."

"Oho! Your brother David! Are you certain?"

"Yes, Kamir. Father has begun to favor him. Can you arrange his disgrace?"

"For this necklace, it will be as you say."

Outside the door, Dargon's mother put her hand across her mouth and hurried away . . .

The next picture showed a white porch overlooking the palace gardens. The King sat in a wicker chair. The Queen, in a yellow robe, stood behind him. Her face looked sad and determined.

"Oh, good! She's going to tell him and save David! I'm wishing for that!"

"Quiet, Amy, so we can hear."

The Queen was speaking rapidly. "Dargon must have taken the other jewels too. Three servants have been wrongly beaten! Do you really think there is a plan to blame David?"

The King sighed. "Yes, I fear it is true." He slapped the arm of his chair. "I suspected Dargon's treachery, but I could never admit it." His bearded face was grim and stormy. "How could twin brothers be so different? They don't even look alike."

"It is hard to believe. Dargon is so clever, so skillful in his evil ways. We must—"

The screen suddenly went blank.

"Hey!" cried Gully. "What's wrong?"

"Please turn it back on," said Amy. "I want to see them protect David."

"I did not turn it off," Mala declared. "There is some kind of interference."

"Mala! Mala!" Both Snoods scuttled frantically into the room. "Instruments show Zarg nearby! Strong reading of Zarg! Eight point one!"

Mala raised a luminous arm. The Snoods grew silent, and a powerful, vibrant change came over the golden man . . .

9
Zarg

Mala's diamond eyes shone like powerful searchlights. His golden skin radiated waves of light. The silence seemed strangely alive. Swirls of glowing particles surged out in all directions.

Several minutes passed. A sour smell like burning rubber filled the air. "Zarg is gone now," said Mala. "Return to your posts."

The Snoods jerked into action. Tentacles twitching, they scuttled from the room.

"What is Zarg?" said Amy. "What's that awful smell?"

"Zarg," said Mala, "is an evil force. At least, that is what he has become. He is invisible, but has an unpleasant odor, especially when he is angered."

"What does he do?" Amy anxiously asked.

"Zarg infects other beings . . . with desire and hatred. As a result, they feel separate and selfish. They do wrong, evil things." Mala sighed. "This spacecraft has instruments that can detect Zarg, and I have learned how to get rid of him . . . at least for a while."

"Why did he come here?" Gully asked.

"Zarg hates goodness. He cannot stand for it to triumph. He must have been attracted by the tests. Dargon's evil deeds had just been exposed. But now we can continue." Mala's eyes glittered, and the screen clicked on . . .

It was night, quiet and eerie. Amy and Gully could see a yellow half-moon, floating above the shadowy palace. A hooded figure emerged. It was David, wearing a dark brown cloak. As he ran, his gold shoes flashed in the moonlight. Keeping close to the wall, he made his way through the garden and slipped into the murky forest . . .

The picture zoomed in to a boy's bedroom. David's parents stood beside the bed. The Queen quietly wept, while the King read from a sheet of pale blue paper.

Dear Mother and Father,
I have decided to leave the palace. If I stayed, it could be very bad for my brother Dargon.
Love, David

On the wide screen, the blue paper blended into the blue sign above a bakery shop. Soldiers were searching the narrow streets of a town. One of them spoke to a hooded figure beside the shop. The figure nodded. He pointed down a dark alley.

The soldier yelled excitedly to the others. They all rushed into the alley. Pulling two gold shoes from under his cloak, the hooded figure put them on . . . and quickly walked away.

Amy raised her hand. "Why did David think it would be bad for Dargon . . . if he stayed in the palace?"

"Yeah," said Gully. "Wouldn't it be worse for David? Wouldn't Dargon do more things to hurt David?"

Mala sighed. "Oh, yes, he probably would. But in the long run, it might have been worse for Dargon. Perhaps David understood that when you hurt someone else, you are really hurting yourself. Please watch."

The next picture showed David, kneeling on green moss, deep in the forest. A shaggy, brown fox huddled beside him, trembling. David had removed a bloody arrow from the animal's hind leg. Now he made a bandage from the lining of his cloak. The fox writhed in pain, but stayed close to David.

Amy shut her eyes and wished very hard for the fox's wound to heal. Then she saw a little bird with a splint on its wing, hopping awkwardly. Its tiny body swayed, lurched, and fell over. David gently picked up the bird and adjusted the splint.

"I can't believe this guy," Gully exclaimed. "First he leaves that great palace, and now he's playing doctor."

"But he's really helping them, Gully." Amy's face was very serious. "That fox knew it, too."

Mala smiled. "That's right. Animals can often sense a person's intentions. Please keep watching."

The fox had risen to his feet. His wound seemed to have healed almost miraculously, but the picture on the screen was changing . . .

Rain drummed down upon a dirty street. Barefoot and wrapped in his dark brown cloak, David humbly held out his hand. People hurried past, ignoring him.

Other beggars, wearing rags the color of ashes, held out their hands too. Some were blind or crippled. Some, old and feeble. Shivering, they crouched in doorways to avoid the rain. If one beggar received a coin, the others flocked around him greedily, like ragged vultures. They pushed and argued, angrily stealing from one another.

Down the street, two beggars were savagely beating an old, one-armed man. They shoved his face down in the gutter, into the dirty water.

"Maybe I can help him," Gully thought. He tried to send some energy and power to the old man, so he could fight back and keep the attackers away.

"Ow!" cried Gully. "My chest! It's all closed up! I can't breathe."

"Calm yourself," said Mala. "Breathe slowly and deeply. Focus on the love in your own heart. That's right. Try to let clear light purify your mind. Good. Now watch the screen."

David rushed to help the one-armed man. He pulled his head up from the gutter. But when he rolled the man over, he was already dead.

10
Treachery

The picture returned to the peach-colored bedroom in the palace. The Queen was lying on the bed with filmy, white curtains. Her face was distorted by pain. She looked very weak. The King and a doctor with his black bag stood beside her.

"This is so sad!" Amy exclaimed. "Even the rich people suffer."

"You are right," said Mala. "There is much suffering. But please watch."

A soldier appeared. "Your Majesty! Prince David was seen wearing a brown cloak . . . begging in the town."

"Send more men," ordered the King. "He must be found. Hurry!"

"Yes, Sire." The soldier briskly saluted and turned on his heels. Rushing out, he almost bumped into Prince Dargon, who was listening at the door.

Dargon faded away, and the streets of the town returned. Soldiers roughly questioned some of the beggars. They answered reluctantly, then laughed behind the soldiers' backs.

"You'll never find him," said a disheveled man with a black eye-patch. "He doesn't come here anymore."

The picture shifted to a long, solemn procession. Crowds of people lined the streets. "She was a fine, generous Queen," an old man declared. Others sadly nodded. Only Prince Dargon did not seem sad.

Walking beside the coffin, the King looked sick and weak. He frowned darkly. "Dargon would not make a good King," he muttered. "I must stay alive until David is found."

"Let's both wish for that," Amy whispered.

"Okay," said Gully. "We should've tried to help the Queen."

The next picture showed Prince Dargon and a tall soldier in a shadowy room. On the table, a lone candle gave out a flickering light. Two jeweled goblets gleamed beside the dancing flame—and two gold shoes.

"You did well to find these shoes, Vytar. I will show them to my father." He paused, smiling maliciously.

"I will tell him they were found in a part of the forest where tigers are known to roam."

Dargon sniffed the air, as if smelling an unpleasant odor. He gave the soldier a handful of silver coins. Then he winked slyly. "When I become King, you will be rewarded more generously."

The soldier grinned. "Thank you, Prince Dargon."

The Prince picked up one of the two goblets. "Let us drink to the glorious future, Vytar."

The soldier hesitated. "Me? Drink with . . . you, your Majesty?"

"Of course. We are partners now. Partners and friends. I reward my friends generously."

Vytar's eyes gleamed. "Thank you, Prince Dargon!"

They both raised their goblets.

The soldier coughed and spluttered. "This drink . . . is very strong, your Majesty."

Prince Dargon laughed. "The essence of mango spirits. A particular favorite of mine. Of course, if it's too potent for you, friend Vytar, I could order some herb tea brought in . . ."

The soldier's face burned. "Uh, no, of course not, Prince Dargon. The drink is excellent."

They both drained their goblets.

The picture shifted to a small, diamond-shaped window overlooking the lawn behind the palace. Prince Dargon peered down. He watched a tall soldier, strolling along a path that led toward the town.

It was Vytar. Amy and Gully could see his smiling face. But his walk was unsteady. His body wobbled, twisting away from the path. Then he fell face down into the grass.

Peering out the diamond-shaped window, Dargon grinned. "Sorry, Vytar," he muttered. "You knew too much. Your reward will have to wait."

Amy turned to Mala. "Is Zarg making Dargon evil? Is there anything we can do?"

"That is for you to decide," Mala replied. "Please watch."

In the peach-colored bedroom, the King was lying on the bed with filmy curtains. His hair was totally white. Servants offered him food on silver trays, but he waved them away. "I have no more use for food," he moaned. "David is dead." Over by the window, the doctor fumbled in his black bag.

"I wished hard for him to get well," said Gully. "But it didn't work."

"You mean, it hasn't worked yet," said Mala.

The next picture showed Prince David, deep in the forest. Before him stood a beautiful deer and four fawns with dark, shiny eyes. The baby deer were thin and trembling. They seemed barely able to stand.

From under his tattered cloak, the Prince pulled out a small loaf of bread. "Here, my friends. This will help you to stay alive. You are five, but I am only one." So saying, he divided the bread among the starving deer.

All of a sudden, the mother deer began to shine with a soft, radiant light. "I am not what I appear," she said. "I am an emanation of the Essence of Loving-kindness. You, Prince David, are needed at the palace." She raised a shiny hoof and touched David's shoulder. Instantly, the Prince was dressed in royal blue garments and a pair of golden shoes.

"Go now," said the deer. "Your father is very ill. He has the same sickness that killed your mother."

Prince David raced through the sunlit forest. His magical transformation seemed to have given him new strength!

Soon he reached the palace gardens. At that moment, Prince Dargon peered down from a high, round window. Recognizing David, he froze in alarm. Then he scowled, sniffing the air. He drew a jeweled dagger from his belt and rushed down the marble stairs.

"Gully! He's gonna kill David!" Amy sprang to her feet and ran up close to the screen.

David moved swiftly down the garden path. His face gleamed in the sunlight. He rushed up to the palace door.

Dargon stood just inside, his eyes gleaming. He raised his jeweled dagger in the air . . .

"No!" Amy shouted. "Watch out, David!"

Halfway through the door, David hesitated. Dargon's dagger slashed the empty air. As he swung, his body pitched forward. Falling to the floor, he lay in shame at David's feet.

"Dargon! Hello. Where is Father? I must see him."

"David! I—I tripped, carrying this dagger. I meant no harm. Father is in his bedroom. He will be pleased to see you."

David raced up the wide, curving staircase . . . and the screen went blank.

"Mala! Mala!" The Snoods scuttled in, waving their tentacles. "Zarg nearby! Even stronger reading! Twelve point five!"

A foul smell like burning rubber filled the air. Mala fixed the Snoods with his diamond eyes. "Ra, bring the chortalizer. Dorg, fetch the bizdle and connect them."

"Yes, Mala!"

"Yes, Mala!"

11

Hatred

Ra scurried in with the chortalizer. Behind him came Dorg. His tentacles held the bizdle—a large crystal cylinder with rainbow sparks dancing inside. The Snoods connected this cylinder to the chortalizer by means of three white cords.

Immediately, the chortalizer's pink screen lit up with a pattern of strange pictures and signs. The rainbow sparks inside the bizdle came together in a bright, swirling column.

"Oh, it's beautiful!" Amy cried.

"*Not to Zarg*," Mala grimly declared. His diamond eyes glittered fiercely. His skin radiated waves of light. The air swirled with surges of glowing, crackling particles . . .

Suddenly, it sounded like hundreds of balloons were being popped! A thick, disgusting smell flooded the room.

"Wow!" said Gully. "I think you got him."

"Yes," said Mala. "Zarg has been severely damaged. He was not expecting that."

"What is Zarg made of?" Gully asked.

"Your language has no word for it," Mala replied. "As I told you, Zarg has become a force for evil. Invisible, with an unpleasant odor. He hates goodness, even though, deep inside, he is like other beings. But his true nature is covered over with a nasty, dirty crust."

Mala continued, "Zarg appears differently on different worlds, attempting to hinder spiritual progress. That is one reason you are being tested. The tests, if successful, will help you when you return to your planet."

Amy's face brightened. "How soon can we go home?"

"When the tests are completed. They were going quite well. That, no doubt, was why the Zarg returned. You had just warned David—and helped to save his life."

Gully ran his fingers through his hair. "You mean David heard Amy . . . when she shouted? That's impossible!"

Mala's eyes shone. "As I said, there is much you do not know about the tests. You can indeed be heard if you speak loudly, and are very close to the screen. But let us continue. David has just reached his father's room. Sit down, won't you?" Mala's eyes flashed—and they could see Prince David, standing beside his father's bed.

". . . and so," the King was saying, "I was certain that you were dead. Dargon must have found your gold shoes and cruelly deceived me. At my death, he would have become King. He must be severely punished."

"No, father. Do not punish Dargon."

"What! David, how can you say that?"

David's face grew sad. "Unfortunately, Father, Dargon's own punishment will come to him. By hurting others, he has already hurt himself."

"But he betrayed you. Dargon must pay for his treacherous deeds now!"

"I feel no hatred for him, Father. I have no desire for revenge. If I speak the truth, may you be cured of your terrible illness!"

Instantly, the King's face shone with health and vigor. His white hair was dark again. Astonished and delighted, he sprang from his bed. "David!" he gasped. "I feel completely well!"

"I think you are, Father. And now, will you please pardon my brother Dargon?"

For a moment, the King frowned. Then his face

brightened. "If you really wish it, I will. It must have been . . . your pure heart that cured me. But how can you bear no ill will toward Dargon?"

"Hatred is a terrible force, Father. I have been among the people, and I have seen its ugly power. I have seen hatred feed upon itself." David's face was sad, but calm and radiant. "Yes, Dargon betrayed me. But to seek revenge is like taking poison. You become infected by negativity."

The King shuddered, staring with awe at his son. "I shall pardon Dargon at once," he declared. "But I shall also give the order for you to become King when I die."

The screen flashed rapidly. Gully and Amy understood that time was passing. Dargon kept slinking about the palace in disgrace. Whenever he saw David, his eyes burned with jealousy and hatred.

David walked alone in the palace gardens. He seemed painfully worried. "All people suffer," he said aloud. "Desire is the cause. They grasp for worldly possessions . . . and cling to them. Their greed is never satisfied. But there must be a way for them to find real happiness. Oh, what a treasure that would be!"

Spying on David through a thick hedge, Dargon

held his nose and grinned. He went directly to the King.

"This is sad to report, dear Father, but it is my duty. Prince David wanders in the garden, talking to himself. He mutters desperately about a treasure that no one can find . . ." Dargon paused, keeping his expression sorrowful and worried.

". . . And though he is alone, he talks to invisible beings, saying that he must help them. Come and see for yourself. I fear he is completely mad. "Yii!" Dargon whirled around, slapping his back. "What was that?"

"I got him that time!" Gully smiled. "C'mon, Amy! Let's send David some power!"

"Good," said Mala. "Now watch the screen."

David was sitting on a flat, red cushion in a little room with bars on the windows. Before him on the floor, Amy and Gully saw a round bowl of fruit.

Dargon entered with the doctor. The old man solemnly took Prince David's pulse. Then he poured some dark yellow liquid into a small cup.

David waved the cup away.

At that moment, the King appeared. "I'm sorry, my son, but this is for the best. You are ill. You must do what the doctor tells you."

"You do not understand," said David. "I only want to find the treasure."

Dargon raised his hand to hide an evil smile.

The doctor bowed to the King. "A very serious case, your Majesty. But this medicine should help." He handed the cup to David, who meekly drank it down.

"You will soon be cured, my son," said the King. But a large tear slipped from his eye. Biting his lip, he left the room.

Dargon turned to David. "I hope you are comfortable, dear brother." He shoved the bowl of fruit closer with his foot. "The treasure will appear to you soon. Eat this nice, fresh fruit and keep on taking your medicine."

Smiling unpleasantly, Dargon added: "Thank you, Doctor Drin, for giving my brother the best of care."

"Yes, Prince Dargon." Bowing low, the doctor left. Dargon followed. A soldier locked the door.

Turning a corner in the hallway, Dargon handed the doctor some gold coins. "Are you still giving him the same drug?" he hissed.

"Yes," the doctor whispered. "But his mind remains quite clear. I have even increased the dose, but he is amazingly strong. His concentration seems to overcome the drug."

"Increase the dose still more," said Dargon.

12

Temptations

The screen flashed rapidly as time passed. David kept sitting on his red cushion, staring straight ahead. His eyes were clear, but intense.

"I'm wishing hard for the drug not to hurt him," said Amy. "Hey, I can tell what he's thinking!"

"So can I," said Gully. "That's really weird!"

David was thinking of life and death—of why we live . . . and what happens when we die. He understood that we are reborn, again and again, in different bodies. *But why?* he wondered. Are we reborn . . . only to suffer again? Oh, he thought fervently, if I could find a way to help beings attain true happiness. What a treasure that would be!

Gully sighed. "That guy is stuck in a rut."

"Wait, Gully! Now he's thinking something new."

We suffer, thought David, because of anger, fear,

and greed. But those are caused by ignorance. The key to the treasure, he thought, must be to break through ignorance, to penetrate deeply into the heart of reality.

"What does *that* mean?" Amy wondered out loud.

"Watch the screen," Mala replied.

David was staring at a bright red apple in his bowl of fruit. It seemed to be looking back up at him—like a round, shiny face.

Behind the apple, David could see a leafy apple tree. Looking deeply at the apple, he could imagine the seed from which the tree had sprung—and the warm sun, helping to make it grow. He also saw the dark, moist earth in which the seed had grown, and the rain which had softened the earth. Behind the rain, he saw great clouds of moisture.

David smiled. The tree, the sun, the clouds, the earth, the seed, the rain . . . They were all there, *inside* the apple. Nothing has a separate self. Each thing depends on every other thing. That was the true face of the apple.

It is the same with people and other beings, he thought. Babies depend upon others. So do the sick and the very old. All our lives, we depend on others much more than we realize.

But that is only in this lifetime. Since we have been

reborn countless times, an endless number of beings have been our mothers—our kind, loving mothers—even beings who seem to be our enemies now.

Those beggars, he thought. The ones who killed the old, one-armed man, who pushed his face in the gutter . . . If I had been born into such poverty and pain, I might easily have acted just as they did . . . To understand all is to love all. We should love them equally—and help them to find happiness . . .

At that moment, the top of the screen suddenly grew dark. A bald head glowed in the darkness. It floated in the air, scowling above Prince David. The head had two sharp horns, gleaming eyes, fanglike teeth. Its expression was ugly and fierce.

Amy stared in horror. "Oh, how awful! Is that Zarg?"

"A part of Zarg has taken that form," Mala replied.

Grinning savagely, the head descended until it almost touched David's head. Grey smoke poured from its nostrils.

David shuddered, but kept on meditating. Visions of gold and sparkling jewels floated before his eyes. A long, lavish banquet table appeared before him. Visions of fine horses, a marble swimming pool, intoxicating

drinks, and other temptations swirled around his head, prying into his thoughts. But David concentrated firmly on loving-kindness.

The evil face grinned. Images of beautiful, smiling women, clad in flowing silk garments, reached out seductively. Then came a vision of David himself, wearing purple robes and a golden crown. He looked handsome and powerful. He stood on a high balcony of the palace. Columns of soldiers in green uniforms marched below.

Again David concentrated on loving-kindness. The visions grew fainter and disappeared.

Scowling darkly and grinding its teeth, the horned head faded away.

David kept on meditating. After a long time, his face began to shine with a calm, quiet happiness.

"Mala!" cried Amy. "David's skin . . . It's starting to look like yours!"

"Yes," said Mala. "It is indeed."

Doctor Drin entered the room, carrying his black bag. "Time for your medicine, Prince David." He poured some dark purple liquid into a cup. "We have a new and stronger medicine today."

Prince David looked up from his cushion. His face shone luminously. He looked at the doctor with clear, intense eyes. "How much gold is Prince Dargon paying you for this?" he quietly said.

The doctor gasped. His eyes bugged out. He dropped the cup. "I . . . uh . . . forgive me, Prince David!" He backed hastily out of the room. A green-uniformed soldier locked the door behind him.

"Gully, it worked! I wished hard for the medicine not to hurt David!"

"So did I, Amy. Let's watch."

On the screen, they could see another royal funeral. The King had died. The people were mourning him.

The picture shifted to a loud, colorful ceremony. Dargon was crowned the new King. Amy and Gully saw him sign an order to make the people pay higher taxes. The treasury was filled with gold, but Dargon told his servants to eat less food.

"You must live on much less," he harshly commanded. Then, sniffing the air, he turned to the Captain of the Guards. "And why do we keep David in that little cell? All he does is stare into space and eat up my food. Execute that lazy fool!"

"Yes, Sire." The Captain, a fat man with gold braid on his uniform, saluted. "Would your Majesty prefer him hanged, burned, or beheaded?"

"Oh, make it a beheading." King Dargon yawned. "We haven't had one of those for a while."

"Yes, your Majesty."

But when the Captain arrived at the little room, he found the door wide open. A soldier sat on David's red cushion, smiling peacefully.

"Guard!" cried the Captain. "Where is the prisoner?"

"I let him go, sir. He showed me the way to find true happiness. He had to leave . . . to show the way to others."

13
The Treasure

The screen flashed and flashed. Years rapidly passed. King Dargon was an old man now, with a curly white beard. "Why do I feel so unhappy?" he grumbled. "Why am I so afraid of sickness and death?"

His face had a terrible, ugly expression. "What will happen when I die?" he muttered angrily. "In my heart, I know that I've been greedy and cruel. Will some awful punishment await me?" Alone in his richly furnished bedroom, King Dargon burst into tears.

He buried his face in his palms. When he raised it again, his eyes were watery and red. "How can David be so happy?" he grumbled. "I hear that he travels as a poor beggar throughout the land. Wherever he goes, the crops grow better and there is prosperity. What does he know that I do not?"

Opening a carved, polished cabinet, King Dargon

drew out a jangling sack. "I shall stack these gold coins," he said. "That always makes me feel better."

He piled the coins in wobbly towers on a marble table. Then he pinched his nose. "What is that foul odor? Can it be that even gold has turned sour for me? Is it a plot to kill me with poisonous gas?"

He ran to the window, threw it open. "No, that is ridiculous. But my food was poisoned just two days ago. It killed my taster. There is a plot. I know it! Well, who cares? I take no pleasure in life anyway."

Seizing a jeweled dagger, King Dargon held it up before the window. Its sharp blade gleamed in the afternoon sun. He gazed at the point as if hypnotized. The picture slowly faded away.

A man with a long, white beard stood at the edge of a village. Dogs began to bark. A group of boys were playing beside a pile of stones. They walked over and surrounded the man.

"Gully! It's David. Look how old he is!"

"Yeah. He's walking with a cane."

"But his face is shining. He looks so happy!"

One of the boys sniffed the air, as if he smelled a strange, foul odor. He ran up to David and knocked his cane away.

Another boy laughed and threw a stone, hitting

David on the shoulder. Still another, a little boy with shaggy hair, yelled: "Attack! Sic 'em!" Some of the dogs rushed at David, snarling viciously.

"No!" cried Amy. "No, don't!"

The dogs snapped at David's legs. The boys, shouting and laughing, threw more stones. David raised his arms to shield his head.

Amy jumped to her feet. She ran right up to the screen. "Stop!" she shouted. "You'll hurt him! Stop!"

Gully blinked in amazement. Amy had gone right into the screen! That couldn't be! But there she was, standing between David and the boys.

"Hey! Wait!" Holding out his arm, Gully rushed to the screen. It wasn't solid at all! It felt like warm, misty air, and it seemed to be sucking him in. "Hey!"

He found himself beside Amy, facing the boys.

Gully turned and saw the dogs, barking and snarling. *We're caught in the middle!* flashed through his mind. He wondered what to do when the boys started throwing stones again.

But the boys just gaped with open mouths. They seemed frozen with fear. One of them dropped to his knees. So did the others.

"We're sorry," said the first boy. "Have you come to punish us?"

Gully took a deep breath. "No," he said.

"Aren't you a young god and goddess?"

"What?" said Amy, laughing.

"Only gods could appear like that . . . out of the air. Have you come from a distant star?"

"No," said Amy. "We were just watching you, and—"

"Oh! You are celestial observers!" A murmur of awe passed through the crowd of boys. "We meant no harm! We promise to be good! Please do not punish us, all-powerful observers!"

Amy giggled. "We were just watching you on a screen."

Gully elbowed her sharply in the ribs. "Yes!" he bellowed in a deep, important voice. "We have been watching you on our observing screen. We do not usually reveal ourselves to . . . ordinary mortals. But you were being very, very bad! Goddess Amy and I were *not* pleased by what we saw. But we will not punish you . . . if you will never do it again."

"Yes, all-powerful observers! Thank you, all-powerful observer-gods!"

"And take those dogs with you," Gully yelled. "Before we change our all-powerful minds!"

"Yes! Yes, at once!" Calling the dogs after them, the boys ran away as fast as they could.

Gully and Amy stood facing David. The old man was calm and radiant. "Thank you," he said. "The dogs were biting."

"Your legs!" cried Amy. "They're bleeding!"

"The wounds are not deep. You arrived in good time." He made a low bow.

"No, don't!" said Amy. *"You're* the one who . . ." Her voice faded away. She and Gully stared at the old man in wonder.

His face seemed to radiate a soft, loving warmth. His eyes shone with quiet happiness. Amy and Gully felt a joy they had never known before.

"It's like being in a circle of magic!" Amy thought. "I feel so free and happy!"

Gully rubbed his eyes and looked at David. "You found the treasure . . . a way to end suffering, didn't you?"

"Yes!" cried Amy. "You found it!" Her eyes were shining. "Will you tell us?"

"I think you already know," said David. "You are able to travel through space, so you must have learned—"

"Oh, no," Amy interrupted. "We're just kids . . . like the ones we scared away."

"Yeah," said Gully. "So will you please tell us?"

David smiled. "This is what I have learned. The

treasure is within us. It is a kind of knowing that cannot be put into words. Think deeply about loving-kindness. You must always wish to help other beings. But you must do so with a pure heart. Never become proud of yourself."

Just then, Amy smelled a foul odor like burning rubber. "Zarg!" she shouted. "Zarg!"

Instantly, she and Gully found themselves in coal-black darkness. It was drafty and eerie and cold.

14
Explanations

"Eee, Gully! Where are we?" Amy's voice echoed strangely in the darkness. She put her arms around his waist. "Help, Gully, help!"

"I can't do anything, Amy. I can't even see!"

Amy started to sob. "Zarg will get us!"

"Don't cry. We'll be okay." Gully's voice made eerie echoes. He didn't sound very confident.

Amy hugged his waist, shaking with sobs. The darkness was scary and cold . . .

Then, all of a sudden, it grew light. They were back in the blue room with Mala! Both Snoods were there too, and the bizdle was connected to the chortalizer. A strong smell of burning rubber floated in the air.

"I had to bring you back," said Mala. "Zarg interfered again."

"I know," said Amy. "I can really smell him."

Dorg blinked his red ring. "We hear you yell *Zarg!* Was good, because Ra not notice reading."

"Not so!" cried Ra. "Was your turn, Dorg, to watch for reading of Zarg!"

"Stop arguing!" Mala fixed the Snoods with his diamond eyes. "We must return these beings to their planet."

"You mean we can go home now?" said Amy. "Are the tests finished?"

"Finished enough," Mala replied.

"But what happened to David?"

"David? He kept helping others to find the treasure. He did so for the rest of his life."

"What about Dargon?" Gully asked.

"Dargon . . . fell deeper and deeper into despair. Finally, he took his own life." Mala sadly shook his head. "But this might interest you. One of the boys you scared away—the little one with shaggy hair—sneaked back just in time to watch you disappear. The boy now thinks that by crying *Zarg!* he will disappear too, but he is afraid to try it."

Amy laughed. Then her face turned serious. "I hope he doesn't," she said. "Saying . . . *that word* . . . might be dangerous."

"I don't see why you gave us the tests," said Gully. "Why did you waste so much time on Amy and me?"

Mala smiled. "First, it was not wasted. Second, time does not exist the way you think of it. Third, I am not merely in this one area of space."

Amy's eyes grew wide. "How . . . Where else could you be?"

Mala laughed like musical chimes. "Do you remember what the mother deer told Prince David?"

Amy closed her eyes. "Yes. That she was an emanation of the Essence of Loving-kindness. I meant to ask you what that was."

"An emanation," said Mala, " is a form sent out by a being. It may resemble the being . . . or look quite different. For example, the way I appear to you now."

Gully gasped. "You mean, there's more of you? I know you changed your shape, but—"

"Yes. I made the shape of this particular emanation look familiar to both of you."

"But . . . but why? How many emanations do you send?"

Mala laughed. "Oh, quite a few. These tests are very important."

Gully looked puzzled. "I still don't understand why you gave us the tests."

Mala's eyes glittered. "I have called them tests, but they were really teachings in disguise. When you and . . . *Goddess Amy* return home, you will not remember what happened, but you will have the teachings inside you. They will help you—and others—for the rest of your lives."

"What did we learn?" Amy asked. "I mean, I guess we learned something, but . . ."

Mala laughed his musical laugh. "More than you might think. When you opened your hearts to the beings on the screen, you were able to help them."

"But why?" Amy looked puzzled. "How did that work?"

Mala smiled. "Pure intention is very strong. Remember how David cured his father?"

Amy nodded.

"Hey," said Gully. "It's like the opposite of angry feelings. They sting like bees."

"That's right," said Mala. "And when you tried to send energy for revenge, your heart closed up painfully. Seeking revenge is like taking poison, as Prince David said."

Mala sighed sadly. "Hatred feeds upon itself. In many cities of your world, there is hatred and blood in the streets. This has far-reaching effects, because all life is connected . . . throughout the entire universe."

Gully grew thoughtful. "What does the universe look like?" he asked.

Mala laughed. "You saw this ship as a little red

bug. Now you know that appearances don't tell the entire story."

Mala's eyes glittered. "You, Gully and Amy, will help others to seek the treasure. Do you remember what Prince David said about loving-kindness?"

"I do," said Amy. "He said to think deeply about it. But you shouldn't be proud of yourself."

"That is right." Mala's eyes shone warmly. "You will develop a selfless concern for the welfare of other beings. You will find inner spaciousness."

"What's that?" said Amy.

"You will understand," Mala replied. "Your mind and heart will become like this ship, which can seem small on the outside but have great spaces within. Now you must go home. The Snoods will beam you back . . . carefully."

"Wait," said Ra, who had been pointing his eyestalks at Gully for some time. "First tell what body shape."

Gully looked puzzled. "Body shape?"

"Yes. When you grockle. After face turns blue."

"Oh, that." Gully burst out laughing. "That was just a joke."

"What mean joke?"

"A joke. You know, something funny. We don't really grockle. I just made it up."

Ra waved his tentacles angrily. "I knew all the time was joke. So ha ha to you."

"Ra," said Dorg, "you are dumber than the bumps on Foofus Five."

Ra blinked his red ring. "You, Dorg, make *shallow* moon crater seem intelligent."

Mala raised a luminous arm. "No more arguing," he commanded. "Our guests must return to their planet."

"Wait," said Amy. "Will we still be the same size?"

"Of course." Mala turned to the Snoods. "Be certain there are no size mistakes when you beam them down."

"Yes, Mala."

"Yes, Mala."

"You'd better hurry," Gully said. "Mom will be worried sick."

"Not in the least," said Mala. "Here, we are outside of your time. Nothing has changed. What were you doing when the Snoods beamed you aboard?"

"Looking for leaves," said Amy. "We were getting two of every kind, so we'd each have one for Mrs. Clearpot. She said to pretend that trees are alien beings. And we were on a secret mission to bring back interesting alien samples."

"Ah." Mala smiled. "Interesting alien samples. We shall have a little fun. Ra, go pick two self-protecting leaves from the red vine taken on Latha Six." Mala chuckled merrily. "Dorg, prepare to return our guests. Apply the appropriate mixture of forget-ray and sleep-ray. Beam the red leaves down with them."

"Yes, Mala."

"Yes, Mala."

15

Alien Samples

"Gully! What happened?" Amy drowsily blinked her eyes.

They were lying in the grass near some blue flowers with bell-shaped blossoms.

Gully yawned. "We must have gone to sleep. Hey! Didn't you see a little red bug somewhere?"

"Yes! Near these flowers. It was jumping all around, I think."

"Well, it's gone now." Gully looked down. "I've got eight leaves—four for each of us. How many did you get?"

"Six. That's funny, I don't remember picking these red ones." She pointed to the self-protecting leaves from Latha Six.

"That gives us plenty. Let's go home. I'm hungry."

"Okay, Gully. I think there's some sugar cookies left."

When they reached the backyard, Gully picked two maple leaves. "Maybe we won't be able to identify all the others, so . . . Amy?" He dashed into the house. Sure enough, she was eating the last sugar cookie.

"Don't spoil your dinner." Mrs. Trent entered the kitchen. "I was saving those cookies for dessert."

Amy looked up, chewing fast. "There's another package in the cupboard, Mom. Behind the crackers."

Mrs. Trent laughed. "I was saving *those* for the weekend. Sometimes, Amy, you're too smart for your own good."

Gully licked his finger to lift a crumb from the table. "Could you help us, Mom? We need to identify some leaves. It's for Mrs. Clearpot."

"I suppose so . . . if it doesn't take too long."

Soon they had labeled all the leaves except the two red ones. "I can't find these anywhere," said Mrs. Trent, paging through *The Favorite Leaves of North America.* "Where did you get them?"

"Rosedale Park, Mom." Amy was pleased she had found something unusual. "We stopped on the way home."

"Well, maybe you'd better skip the red ones. Haven't you got enough without them?"

"Yes, but Mrs. Clearpot wanted *interesting* leaves. And these sure are interesting." Amy stroked one with her finger. "It's soft and fuzzy, like a peach."

"Maybe Mr. Dryfield will know," said Gully. "He loves flowers. We can ask him tomorrow, on the way to the bus."

The next morning, when they reached Mr. Dryfield's yard, Elmer didn't come bounding out to greet them as usual. He crouched on the lawn, holding his head very low.

Mr. Dryfield rushed out the front door. "Hi, Amy. Hi, Gully. You kids see anyone picking flowers in my yard?"

"No, Mr. Dryfield," Amy replied.

"Well, one of my prize pink roses is missing." Mr. Dryfield narrowed his eyes. "Elmer's all upset. I think he saw the thief."

Gully shrugged. "Maybe a bee stung him or something." He held up one of the red leaves. "Could you please do us a favor? We've got to identify this for school."

Mr. Dryfield examined the leaf. "Sorry, I've never

seen anything like that. It certainly is soft and silky. Where did you find it?"

"Rosedale Park," Amy said proudly.

On the bus, Gully asked Gerry Flathers about his punishment, but he still wouldn't say. He just shuddered and shook his head. But when they entered the auditorium for the school meeting, Gerry politely said "Good morning, sir" to Mr. Wilkins.

Today Mrs. Clearpot was wearing a pale blue dress, so her round body looked like a blue balloon instead of a silver one. She squinted her eyes and smiled a sugary smile. "Well, children, did you remember your secret mission? Samples from alien trees? I hope you got some exciting ones! Let's see, now . . ." Her glasses glinted in the light. "Let's have Gerald Flathers show us his leaves first. Gerald?"

For a moment, nothing happened. Then Gerry, holding a small paper bag, walked slowly up to the front of the room. One by one, he held up his leaves. "Oak . . . maple . . . uh, elm . . . ash . . . walnut."

"Excellent, Gerald!" Mrs. Clearpot chortled with approval. "Five little hands from five different friends, hee hee. You may go back to your seat now."

Her shiny glasses scanned the room. "Next, let's have . . . Amy Trent. What interesting leaves did you bring us, dear?"

Amy walked up and stood beside Mrs. Clearpot. "Here," she said, holding out a clear plastic bag.

"My, how exciting! And their names?"

Amy held up each leaf, naming it correctly. But then, for no reason at all, she suddenly thought of tentacles—long, silvery tentacles, reaching out from Mrs. Clearpot's round body. Amy began to giggle.

"What's so funny, dear?"

Amy looked confused. "It's . . . it's this!" she blurted, pulling a red leaf from her pocket.

"Why, how nice! An *extra* sample. You certainly fulfilled your mission. Now tell us the . . . Here, let me see that."

Amy gave her the leaf.

"My, this *is* an interesting sample. A nice, deep red and so velvety smooth. You *do* know its name, don't you, dear?"

"No, Mrs. Clearpot. What is it?"

"Why, uh let me see. Just a moment." Mrs. Clearpot pinched the leaf between two fingers, squeezing and pulling. "It's a . . . Ouch! I didn't see those prickles. *Ouch!*" She looked like she'd picked up a poisonous spider.

Laughter rang out. The red leaf swooped and fluttered to the floor. Mrs. Clearpot cautiously bent down to pick it up. But at that moment—Amy later told

Gully she heard it very clearly—the leaf made a vicious little snarl.

"Eee-ah!" Mrs. Clearpot gasped and fainted dead away. Mr. Wilkins rushed forward too late. Her heavy body slumped, senseless, to the floor.

The red leaf was never identified. They put it in a glass jar, but it mysteriously disappeared. No one saw this happen. It self-destructed on the way to the testing lab. Mrs. Clearpot muffled a squeal when they called to say that the jar was empty.

Amy was sorry her red leaf had scared Mrs. Clearpot and made her faint. But she had to smile, remembering the teacher's expression when she heard that vicious little snarl!

Gully never did find *his* red leaf, even though he turned his pockets inside out several times. But from that day on, he and Amy stopped teasing other kids in school. If anyone was picked on or made fun of, they both tried to distract the other kids so they'd stop. And late one afternoon, much to his own surprise, Gully found himself talking to Amy about loving-kindness.